Dan and Lotta Höjer

Heart of Mine

A Story of Adoption

R&S BOOKS

Stockholm New York London Adelaide Toronto

For Tua

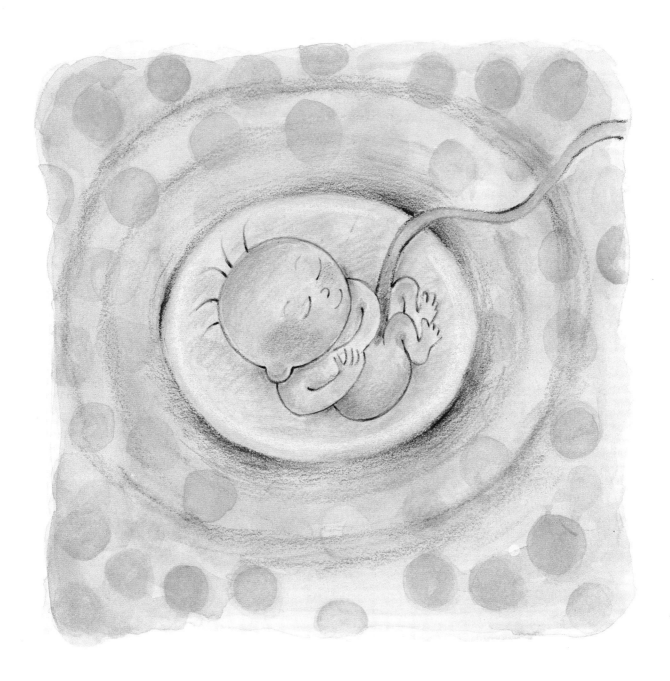

Once a little girl grew in her mommy's belly in a land far away. It was nice and warm in there. She grew big and strong; she got fingers and toes, nails and hair. And finally she was ready to come out of the tummy, out into the world.

Her daddy and mommy wanted to take care of their little girl.
But they could not. They needed help to find a new family for her.

At the same time, another mommy and daddy were longing
and waiting on the other side of the world. They longed for a
child to take care of and love. They were waiting to become a
family.

Their child grew and grew. Not in the mommy's tummy,
but in the daddy and mommy's thoughts and hearts.

One day the phone rang in the home
of the parents who longed and
waited.

"Your little girl has been born!
She is in a land far away.
Come as soon as you can!"

First they were quiet.
For a little while, time
stopped. Then they began
to laugh, cry, and shout.
And then they cried some more.

"We have a daughter! A little girl!"

They held each other and danced around the apartment.

They repeated the words over and over: "A daughter!"

The next day the sun was shining for the first time in many weeks. When they looked out the window, everything seemed different. It was a whole new world.

Now *you* are in it, they thought.

They tried to picture her. What is she doing right now?
Is she sleeping? Is she laughing? Is she eating? And they
sent their thoughts through the night. Sweetie! Soon we
will be with you.

Her name was Tu Thi. The parents wrote it on a piece of
paper over and over again. And they tasted the name in
their mouths. Tu Thi – how pretty!

They told everyone about her. Their parents, their
sisters and brothers, and all their friends. And everyone
longed to meet her right away.

Before Grandma hung up, she said, "Do you know what? Tu Thi was born on Valentine's Day!"

Of course, thought the parents. She is the child of our hearts.

She is what we wanted most of all.

They couldn't think of anything except Tu Thi. When it was time to eat, they weren't hungry. When it was time to sleep, they weren't sleepy. They thought only of their little daughter, who waited for them on the other side of the world.

And at night they met her in their dreams.

One day a letter came with curly handwriting on the envelope.
They opened the letter, and there was her picture: Spiky hair.
Blue shirt. Round cheeks and a tiny little mouth.

They made copies of the photograph and hung it up all
over their apartment. And every night, when they went to bed,
they kissed her good night.

They bought children's clothes and a baby blanket. They cleaned the house and put together a crib in the bedroom. They bustled about for several weeks and prepared everything. When they returned from their long journey, there would be three of them.

They were ready to leave. A huge airplane flew them high over the clouds straight through the night – to the other side of the world. To the place where their daughter had been born.

Everything was so different than it was at home. But right away they loved the land they'd come to. They loved the unfamiliar smells, the ring of thousands of bicycle bells, the moist heat, and the people.

Then the big day came. The day when they were going to meet their daughter for the very first time.

In their nicest clothes, they went to the house where Tu Thi lived. There was the bed that she had slept in and her first toy – a little woolen dog. But the new parents saw only her dark eyes, her small fingers, and her hair, which stood straight up. And she smelled delicious.

The foster mother who had taken care of Tu Thi placed the toy dog in her arms, gave her a hug, and waved goodbye.

Finally, they could hold her.

First she looked at them with concern. But when the parents sang a song for her about an eentsy, weentsy spider, the little girl laughed. The song was in a language she didn't recognize, and the new people smelled different from her foster mother. But she liked the melody, and soon she slept in her mommy's arms, which were warm and nice.

That night the three of them slept in the same bed. Tu Thi woke up and ate some oatmeal. She peed and got a new, dry diaper.

The next day they played and danced to music, which the parents had brought from home.

They hugged their little girl and kissed her all over. They did everything again and again until she laughed so her belly jumped up and down. Love grew big and strong in Tu Thi's mommy and daddy. Slowly the three got to know each other before they began the long journey home.

Then they sat on the plane. The parents whispered in her ear. They told her about the silence in the country far away. About ice-blue winter days, birch trees, and light summer evenings. About green grass that tickles under your toes.

Tu Thi slept almost the whole way, while they flew high above the clouds, straight through the night, halfway around the world. Home to their family, who stood waiting in the airport.

On the second day in the new country, the parents carried
Tu Thi up to the top of a hill. There they told her about
their dreams and secrets.

"This is where we will live. This is where you will grow
up. From now on we belong together," said the daddy.

"How lucky that you were the one," said the mommy
and hugged her daughter.

Then they went home and played and made oatmeal for Tu Thi.

And that's how it happened that the little girl, who grew
ready for life in her mommy's tummy, got a mommy and a
daddy on the other side of the world. A mommy and a daddy
to grow up with and love and be loved by. Forever after.
And her mommy and daddy's greatest wish came true.

There are still continents and oceans, rivers and high mountains between Here and the Country far away. But it never takes Tu Thi and her parents more than a few seconds to cross them in their thoughts and dreams.

Rabén & Sjögren Bokförlag, Stockholm
www.raben.se

Translation copyright © 2001 by Rabén & Sjögren Bokförlag
Text copyright © 2000 by Dan and Lotta Höjer
Illustrations copyright © 2000 by Lotta Höjer
All rights reserved
Originally published in Sweden by Rabén & Sjögren under the title *Hjärtat mitt*
Library of Congress catalog card number: 00-135407
Printed in Denmark
First American edition, 2001
ISBN 91-29-65301-0